Diabetes Doesn't Stop Maddie!

Sarah Glenn Marsh
illustrated by Maria Luisa Di Gravio

Albert Whitman & Company
Chicago, Illinois

For my sister Lindsey, my friends at The Honest Exchange,
and all the other type 1 warriors out there:
I see you, and you're fierce—SGM

For Simone—MLDG

Library of Congress Cataloging-in-Publication data is on file with the publisher.

Text copyright © 2020 by Sarah Glenn Marsh
Illustrations copyright © 2020 by Albert Whitman & Company
Illustrations by Maria Luisa Di Gravio
First published in the United States of America in 2020 by Albert Whitman & Company
ISBN 978-0-8075-4703-8 (hardcover)
ISBN 978-0-8075-4704-5 (ebook)

Printed in China
10 9 8 7 6 5 4 3 2 1 HH 24 23 22 21 20 19

Design by Rick DeMonico

For more information about Albert Whitman & Company,
visit our website at www.albertwhitman.com.

"Time for school!" Dad calls on Monday morning.

Maddie pulls the covers over her head.

She loves school, but it's her first day back since she learned she has type 1 diabetes. Her body stopped making insulin, which turns sugar in food into energy.

As she checks her morning blood sugar and gives herself insulin, her little brother, Alex, peeks in. "Can I play with your phone too?"

"No, silly," she answers. "This isn't a cell phone. It's an insulin pump. Remember how my pancreas stopped making insulin? This delivers it straight into my body instead."

"What's that?" he asks as Maddie quickly inserts a fresh CGM sensor into her arm.

"This is my continuous glucose monitor," Maddie tells him.

"Ouch," he says, rubbing his arm. "Does that hurt?"

"Not once it's in. Then I can't even feel it. The CGM gives me blood sugar readings so I know how much insulin I need, but Dad says it's important to always listen to my body when I feel thirsty or shaky—"

"Because that means your blood sugar is too high or too low!" Alex finishes.

Maddie needed to learn a lot about how to manage her care before being ready to go back to school.

"Let's get your supplies ready, Maddie Magnificent!" Dad says.

Maddie grabs juice boxes, granola bars, and a glucagon kit in case of low blood sugars, extra batteries for her insulin pump, and an extra glucose meter and testing strips in case something happens to her CGM.

She knows she has everything she needs. But Maddie still wants to hide in her closet.

She doesn't feel like Maddie Magnificent today.

She's afraid of stares and questions. She wants to be treated like everyone else.

Her dad cooks her favorite breakfast: waffles!

"Sixty carbs for those," he says.

Maddie tells her insulin pump how many grams of carbohydrates, nutrients that give our bodies energy, are in her meal. This will let her pump know how much insulin to give before breakfast.

"See, you've got this!" says Dad.

Maddie almost smiles. But she's busy wondering how she will hide her insulin pump during lunch. She tugs her long shirt, hoping it will help.

Her classmates cheer when she walks in, especially her best friend, Brianna.

"What did you have?" Lee asks. "Was it strep? Chicken pox?"

Maddie just shrugs and sits with Brianna.

At lunchtime, Maddie's hands start to sweat as she uses her pump.

A third grader passing by says, "Hey! We can't have cell phones in school!"

"It's not a cell phone," she says. But he keeps staring. "This is an insulin pump for my type 1 diabetes."

Now other kids are stopping to stare too.
"What's diabetes? Is it contagious?"
"Does this mean you can't have Halloween candy anymore?"
"Can you still play at recess?"
Maddie blinks back tears. She wants to go home.

"She can do everything you can!" Brianna chimes in. She knows Maddie is shy. "No, diabetes isn't contagious, and yes, she can still eat candy—if she takes her insulin."

Brianna sits next to Maddie. "My sister's pump is like that," she says. "Hers is blue."

Maddie had forgotten that Brianna's sister has type 1 also. It's good to know there are others just like her.

"She checks her blood sugar with a glucose meter," Brianna adds. "But she's thinking about getting a CGM too."

"Thanks for answering those questions for me," Maddie says.

Talking about type 1 with Brianna is nice, but Maddie is not ready to share with everyone else.

In art class on Wednesday, her CGM gives a noisy *beep*. Uh-oh! Her blood sugar is going too low. Everyone stops painting to watch.

Maddie freezes. She needs some sugary juice, but she doesn't want to drink it in front of everyone. With sweaty, shaky hands, she takes out a small juice box.

"How come she gets juice? No fair!" Sophie huffs.

Maddie's cheeks turn pink.

"She needs something sugary to help her feel better," Luis explains.

How does he know? Maddie wonders.

On Saturday, Maddie has her first soccer game since being diagnosed.

"Nervous, Maddie Magnificent?" Dad asks as she packs a snack.

Maddie shakes her head. "I have a plan." She holds up a granola bar. The combination of sugar and carbohydrates will help prevent her blood sugar from going too low during the game.

During warm-up, Maddie passes the ball to Luis.

"Heads up, your CGM's showing," he says, glancing at her arm. "My abuelo has the same one."

Maddie's eyes widen. "He has type 1 too?"

"For sixty years!" Luis answers as two of their teammates run by.

"What's that? Maddie, are you a robot?"

Maddie doesn't answer. Her mouth has gone dry. Not this again!

"Hey Maddie, let's go get some water," Luis says quickly.

"My abuelo doesn't like people asking about his CGM either," Luis confides.

"Thanks. It's not easy explaining to everyone," Maddie says. She likes that she can be herself and manage her diabetes around Luis. "Want to sit with me and Brianna at lunch on Monday?"

Luis nods and smiles.

On Sunday, Maddie, Alex, and Dad go for ice cream.
Maddie counts carbs and gives herself the correct dose
of insulin without any help.

"How was the first week, sweetheart?" Dad asks.

Maddie takes a deep breath. "It was hard. Kids asked a lot of questions. But next week will be better. I know what to say now, and I have friends to help too."

Dad gives her a hug.

On Monday, Luis brings cupcakes to share!
"It's thirty-six grams of carbs," Luis says as Maddie takes one.

Maddie doesn't try to hide her insulin pump this time. Not with Brianna and Luis beside her.

Lee joins them too, glancing at Maddie's pump. "How does that thing work?"

Taking a deep breath, Maddie looks at Brianna. Then she starts to explain. "Well, it's easy when you take it a step at a time…"

Life is sweet with type 1 diabetes. It's even sweeter when sharing with friends.

Author's Note: You Are Not Alone

When I went to a doctor for a minor ailment at age twenty, I had no idea I'd be walking out with a life-altering diagnosis of type 1 diabetes. Perhaps I had some of the symptoms Maddie experiences in this story, but if so, I didn't notice; after all, college life is exhausting—who isn't tired and thirsty after running between classes? I was terrified of needles, and I felt a lot of awful things in those first months—but luckily for me, the one thing I didn't feel was alone. Understanding and having answers to so many of my questions were right beside me, in the bedroom next to mine.

My younger sister, Lindsey, had been diagnosed with type 1 diabetes around age seven. Growing up, I'd watched her go from daily insulin injections and testing her blood sugar regularly with a glucometer to using an insulin pump and wearing a CGM. She has always been what I consider "tough"—meaning, unafraid of needles and willing to try new things without worry, even participating in some type 1 research trials. Thanks to Lindsey, I already knew how to work an insulin pump, and different ways to treat low and high blood sugar. I also knew that type 1 didn't have to hold me back from traveling, trying new foods, or pursuing my dreams; all it meant was extra steps in my daily routines to take care of myself. In some ways, at the time of my diagnosis, I was ahead of the game with all my diabetes knowledge.

But in others, I wasn't, because there was one important thing I didn't know: everyone's diabetes is different! I'm still afraid of needles and find them painful, while they don't really bother my sister. Oatmeal that spikes my blood sugar may not spike hers. We need different amounts of insulin every day. Our bodies respond best to different treatments for our low blood sugars. We wear different pumps and different CGMs. (It's really fun to compare and share technologies!)

Being in the same family, I never would have guessed that we would have different needs and strategies for treating our diabetes, yet every body is unique. This is why it's so important to never judge a fellow person with type 1 for taking care of themselves in a different way that they and their doctor have agreed upon, and it's also why type 1 can sometimes feel so isolating. The best thing to do when feeling lost or alone with this disease is to get involved in the type 1 diabetes community, where there is plenty of friendship and understanding to be found. In such a large group of people, you're bound to meet someone with similar experiences who can help you figure out whatever challenge you're facing, or just lend a sympathetic ear.

Life is short, but it can also be sweet. Eat the cupcake. (Just take insulin for it first.)

Additional Resources

American Diabetes Association: http://www.diabetes.org/
Beyond Type 1: https://beyondtype1.org/
Children With Diabetes: http://childrenwithdiabetes.com/
Juvenile Diabetes Research Foundation: http://www.jdrf.org/
Project Blue November: http://www.projectbluenovember.com/

About Type 1 Diabetes Mellitus, or Juvenile Diabetes

You likely know of someone with type 1 diabetes; some celebrities and athletes are open about their diagnoses. But many people also know someone closer to them, often a child, who has diabetes. Although only 5 percent of all diabetes is type 1 (versus type 2), 1.25 million Americans have type 1, including 200,000 youth, according to the 2017 National Diabetes Statistics Report. Each year, 40,000 people (roughly 18,000 youth) will be newly diagnosed with type 1 in the United States, and the rates keep rising.

Type 1 diabetes is an autoimmune disorder where your immune system mistakenly attacks the islet cells of the pancreas, for reasons that are still largely unknown. Consequently, your body cannot produce enough insulin (a hormone), which regulates levels of glucose (a sugar) in the bloodstream and helps the body use glucose from your food for energy. Without insulin, cells starve, and the body gets sick. Much research is being devoted to learning why this happens. Unfortunately, there are no proven prevention strategies (but, on the flip side, you didn't cause it—no matter what you ate!).

Individuals with type 1 diabetes can be treated only by taking insulin (by injection or insulin pump) multiple times per day, with doses calculated based on the carbohydrate content in food and on blood glucose readings. Blood glucose levels must be carefully monitored throughout the day (and night!) to protect against potentially life-threatening severe low blood glucose (hypoglycemia, which can lead to seizures or coma) and persistent high blood glucose (hyperglycemia, which can lead to diabetic ketoacidosis, or DKA).

Children will need direct help or indirect supervision from responsible adults in their homes and schools to stay safe with their care, based on their maturity levels. Although diabetes requires constant attention, persistent management will pay off with lifelong health benefits and the possibility of doing almost anything!

Christine Burt Solorzano, MD
Pediatric Endocrinologist
University of Virginia Children's Hospital